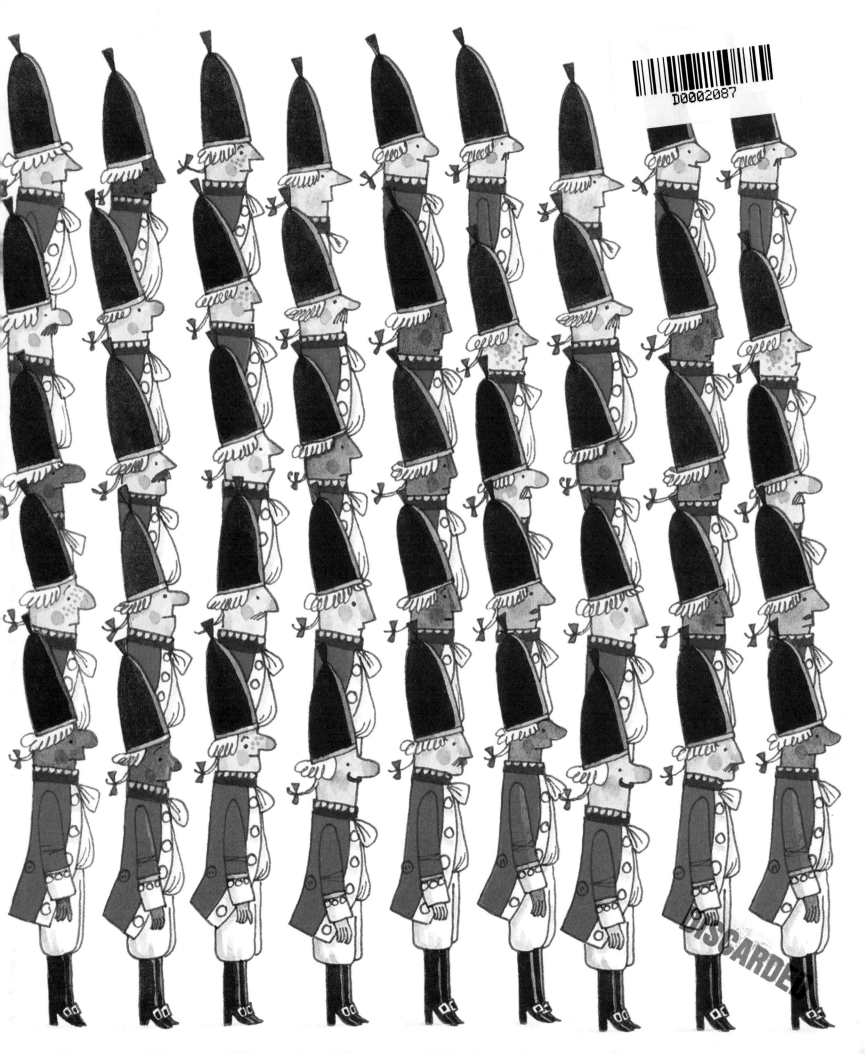

For my son Theo,
who eats everything in sight

P.B.

For Humphrey Hall

D.R.

The illustrations in this book were made with watercolors,
pen, and ink on Arches paper.

Cataloging-in-Publication Data has been applied for and
may be obtained from the Library of Congress.

ISBN: 978-1-4197-2312-4

Text copyright © 2015 Peter Bently
Illustrations copyright © 2015 David Roberts

Published by arrangement with Andersen Press, one of the Penguin Random
House Group companies. Originally published in the United Kingdom in 2015.

Printed and bound in China

10 9 8 7 6 5 4 3 2 1

Abrams Books for Young Readers are available at special discounts when
purchased in quantity for premiums and promotions as well as fundraising or
educational use. Special editions can also be created to specification. For details,
contact specialsales@abramsbooks.com or the address below.

ABRAMS The Art of Books
115 West 18th Street, New York, NY 10011
abramsbooks.com

The PRINCE and the PORKER

Written by
PETER BENTLY

Illustrated by
DAVID ROBERTS

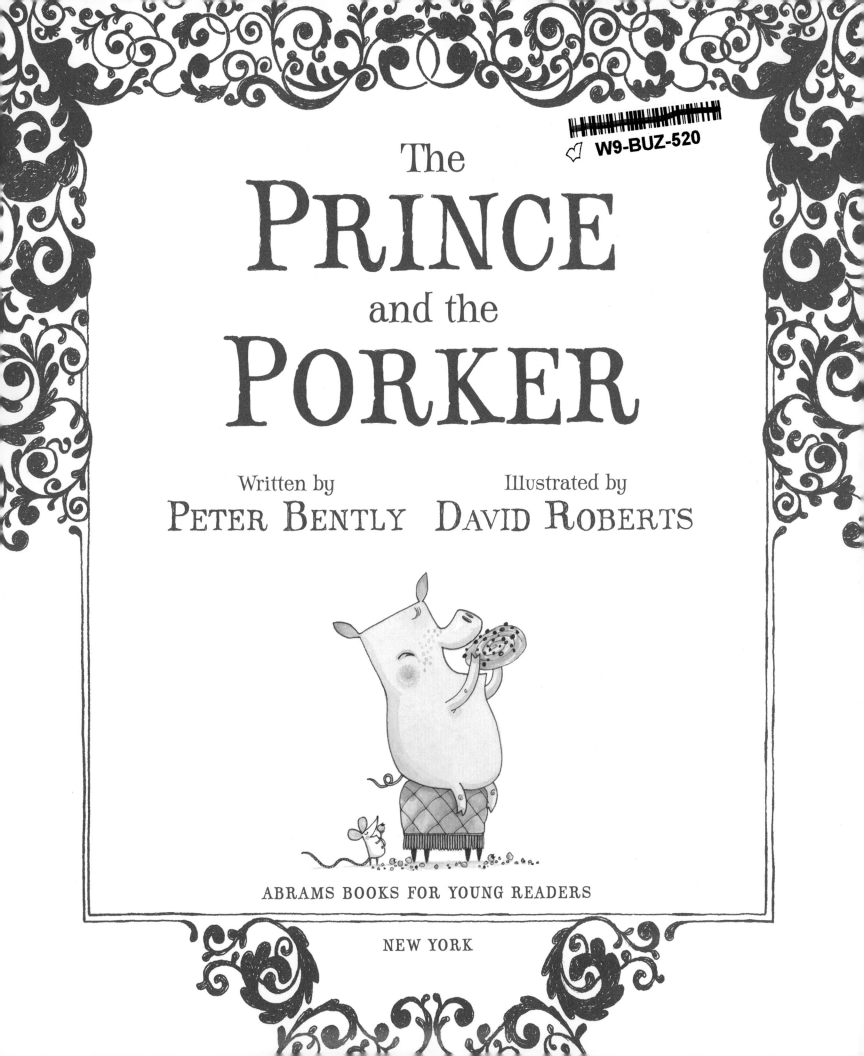

ABRAMS BOOKS FOR YOUNG READERS

NEW YORK

Pignatius was passing the palace one day
when he saw ten fresh buns left to cool on a tray.
"Mmm," thought Pignatius. "I'm sure that it's fine
if I try just one bun. That still leaves them nine."

"Delicious!" he said as he chomped on that bun.
And the next—and the next—until soon there were none.

"I wonder," he thought, "if they've made any more?"

"I think I'll just check." And he crept through the door . . . .

Pignatius was eyeing a big jar of cream
when the cook scurried in and let out a huge scream.
"He's eaten the prince's fresh buns, every one!"
"Oops!" thought Pignatius. "I think I'd best run!"

He fled from the kitchen and into the hall, which was being prepared for a banquet and ball.

"STOP!" cried the cook as he nipped past the chairs and made his escape up the great flight of stairs.

"I wonder who sleeps in this chamber?" he said,
as he entered a room with a four-poster bed.
The bedroom was splendid.
The pig was impressed.
He chuckled, "There's even a dressing-up chest!"

He had to admit that he cut a fine dash
with his buckles and breeches
and blue satin sash.
"What larks!" he exclaimed as he added a wig
that hid half his face (it was slightly too big).

He admired his reflection
from front, back, and side.
But what was that noise
on the landing outside?

Then the cook and the butler, six maids and a groom,
plus several footmen burst into the room!
Pignatius grinned nervously, eyeing the crowd,
but to his astonishment . . .

...everyone bowed!

The butler said, "Pardon this dreadful intrusion!
Your Highness, I fear that there's been some confusion.
The cook is mistaken, it's quite clear to see.
Now, what does Your Highness desire for his tea?"

"Gosh!" thought Pignatius. "They think I'm the prince."
And he said, "For my tea, I'd like . . . chocolate and quince!"
"At once," bowed the butler. The pig thought, "What fun!"
And he cheekily added, "And bring a fresh bun!"

Then he ordered:
"A cinnamon tart,
nice and hot,
and two jelly trifles—
the biggest you've got!
Three tubs of syllabub,
four treacle rolls,
five figgy puddings with
custard (six bowls).
Seven gateaux,
eight gooseberry pies,
nine fondant fancies
of extra-large size.
And lastly," the pig said,
"I almost forgot—
ten gallons of cream!"

And he gobbled the lot.

Then it was time to inspect the new guard,
who were neatly lined up by the gate in the yard.

"Now for more fun!" thought the mischievous hog,
and he ordered the soldiers to hop like a frog.
He made them do cartwheels and gallop and leap,
till they all ended up in a big tangled heap.

Then he blew the head gardener's pumpkin to bits!

And startled two duchesses out of their wits.

"Now," said Pignatius, "I fancy more grub.
Bring me some sweets in a very large tub."
Pignatius was munching a mouthful of mints
when into the hall strode . . .

...the genuine **prince!**

The butler took hold of Pignatius's wig,
then pulled it, and gasped,
"Goodness gracious . . .

. . . . A PIG!"

The cook cried,
"I knew that I wasn't mistaken!
I'll have him for sausages,
gammon, and bacon!"

She turned to the
prince as he stood
in the hall
and told how Pignatius had
hoodwinked them all.

"Do you seriously mean," said the prince with great glee,
"that you truly believed that
this porker was ME?"

"Pig," he declared, "you've
been nothing but trouble.
However, I might have
some use for a double!"

Pignatius now gets to eat chocolate and quince
and sleeps in a chamber next door to the prince.

But once every week,
he has had to agree
that he'll dress as the prince
and go down to have tea
with that terrible dragon . . .

. . . the prince's Aunt Alice,
when she comes every Thursday
to visit the palace!